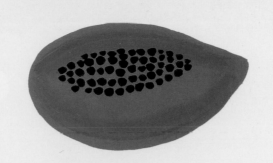

Juan's Sweet and Spicy Memory

About the Author
Hee Jung Yoon began writing novels and children's books after studying Korean literature in college. She has also authored *My Mom, Mrs. Bo Yim Choi, The Life Story as Told by Nature, When I Met Socrates, A Strange Man, Earth, Are You Alright?, Five-Thousand-Year-Old Art that Surprised the World,* and *Myeong-Shim-Bo-Gam,* among others.

About the Illustrator
Christopher Corr was born in London and studied graphic design at Manchester Polytechnic and illustration at the Royal Academy of Arts. He has won art awards from several organizations and is currently illustrating children's books, stamps, and magazines. The illustrations' vivid tone and simplistic characters bring out the sentiments of South America.

Tantan Publishing Knowledge Storybook *Juan's Sweet and Spicy Memory*

www.TantanPublishing.com

Published in the U.S. in 2016 by TANTAN PUBLISHING, INC.
4005 w Olympic Blvd., Los Angeles, CA 90019-3258

ISBN: 978-1-939248-12-1

Printed in Korea

Juan's Sweet and Spicy Memory

Written by Hee Jung Yoon   **Illustrated by Christopher Corr**

✿ TanTan Publishing

"Hola"

My name is Juan and I live in Mexico.
"Hola" means "hello" in Spanish.
My family owns a taco restaurant in the market.
You are just in time for tomorrow's big festival,
called "Cinco de Mayo."
"Cinco de Mayo" is a festival celebrating a battle
on May 5, 1862 that was won by a small Mexican
Army of 2000 against a large invading French
Army of 6000. It was a remarkable victory! I am
already too excited to sleep.
Would you like to go with me to Cinco de Mayo?

3

It is the day of the festival.
It looks like Grandma and Mom are making tortillas.
I can hear them beating the dough,
and the smell of baked tortillas fills the entire house.
"Oh no, I will be late if I don't hurry."
I quickly get ready and go into the kitchen.

Tortilla

A tortilla, made from corn, is the staple starch for Mexican people, just like potatoes are for Americans. Corn is soaked in water and ground using a millstone, then flattened in a round and wide shape before toasting it. You can wrap a tortilla around vegetables, meat, or seafood. It can also be fried and eaten crispy, dipped in sauce, or added to a soup dish.

I eagerly sit down at the table.
I try the chicken tostadas on a
fried tortilla.
"Yum, it is crunchy and delicious
as always!"

After eating quickly, I grab my
festival hat and go outside.
My friend Pancho and I have
made plans to meet at the plaza
early this morning.
I am excited to show off the hat I
have been working on for the last
couple of days.

◈◉ Meals in Mexico

People in Mexico eat four meals a day. In the morning they eat a light
breakfast with bread and coffee or juice. Then around 11 AM they eat a
quick sandwich or a tortilla dish. The most abundant meal is lunch, which is
around 3 PM. Around 8 or 9 in the evening, they have a light dinner.

On my way, a neighbor gives me a ride to the plaza
in his car.
The path to the plaza from the village is surrounded
by cornfields.
"Juan, look at all those valuable corn."
"Sir, what is so valuable about the corn we eat
every day?"
The man laughs loudly.
"Corn is valuable, because it always keeps people
full! A along time ago, there was even a corn god."
The man shares many interesting stories about corn
before dropping me off at the plaza.

◆ ◇ **Mexico's god of corn**

For seven thousand years, corn has been the
main food in Mexico.
Therefore, corn represents life. Legend has it
that a corn-resembling god created humans
using dough made from corn powder.

9

Wow, the plaza is already filled with an exciting and festive atmosphere. From men wearing wide-brimmed hats, called sombreros, and ladies dressed in fancy traditional clothing, to tourists who came to watch the festival, there are many people. "Juan, over here, here!" Pancho waves his hands at me from the other side of the plaza.

We watch the festival eagerly.
We must have walked around too much because we become hungry.
So we buy and eat a round, wide, and flat pastry called a coyota, along with lemonade. Coyotas have a sweet filling in the middle and are similar to turnovers.
Just then, the tourists next to us try to ask us something. "Taco? Taco?"
I think they want to eat tacos.
"Juan, let's take them to your taco restaurant!"
Pancho whispers in my ear.
It is true that our restaurant's tacos are delicious.

I lead the tourist family to my dad's taco restaurant.
"Dad, I think these tourists want to taste tacos."
My dad skillfully makes the tacos in front of the tourists.
He folds a tortilla in half and fries it, then adds
plenty of meat and beans, thinly sliced lettuce,
and cheese.
"The best Mexican dish is a taco, no matter what!
Please tell me if you want to add other toppings.
Tacos are delicious with anything."
The tourist family nods their heads even though
they do not understand.

My dad brings out some sauce for the tourist family.

"You can't get the real taste of Mexico by eating a taco all by itself.
You have to try it with some sauce called salsa Mexicana."

The family hesitates at first, but then pours the sauce on the tacos.

Suddenly, the little boy sticks out his tongue and begins panting.

He must have tasted the hot spices from the salsa Mexicana.

I quickly bring him a glass of water.

◈ **Mexico's main condiment:
Salsa Mexicana**

People in Mexico eat tacos with sauces
that come in a variety of flavors: spicy,
delicate, or refreshing, to name a few.
The most well-known sauce is salsa
Mexicana.
It is a spicy sauce made with ingredients
like tomatoes, onions, chili peppers, and
garlic. Salsa means sauce.

Everyone who tries Mexican food for the first time always says it is spicy.

So it might be difficult to eat at first, but once you get used to it, you will love the spicy taste of Mexican cuisine. My dad brings out all the foods he has made with tortillas.

"The one that is toasted and rolled around the filling with a sauce is an enchilada. A quesadilla is like a grilled sandwich, except it's made with tortillas instead of bread. Dip the chip-like nachos into the melted cheese."

"Dad, please bring out the rectangular burritos, too."

Before we know it, the table is covered with tortilla dishes. I notice that the tourist boy keeps looking at my hat while he is eating.

He must think my hat is cool, too.

My family and the tourist family quickly
become acquainted.
Although we do not speak the same language,
it doesn't matter.
Pancho and I guide them to several attractions.
First, we go to the art museum to see
a famous Mexican mural.
The mural has vivid drawings of Mexico's history.
The tourist family takes a close look at the mural.
We leave the museum and return to the plaza.
At the plaza, we have a great time playing tag and
taking pictures, with our arms around
each other's shoulders.

Watching the tourist family having a great time
reminds me of our family vacation last year.
My family drove to Tequila village.
There were an infinite number of cacti as tall as me.
People cut these tall cacti to make alcohol.
I also remember crying after getting pricked by
the sharp spines while running around the cacti.
I locate Tequila village in the travel book and point
it out to the tourist family.
"You must go here!" I say and give a thumbs up.

The Land of Cacti (Cactus is singular. Cacti is plural)

In the highlands of Mexico, people grow a lot of corn and cacti. There are about 2000 different kinds of cacti in Mexico. The Aztecs, the ancestors of the Mexican people, believed that the gods told them to build a nation where they saw an eagle holding a snake while perched on a cactus. The legendary eagle is pictured in the center of the Mexican flag.

All that walking makes us hungry again.
My stomach rumbles so loudly that everyone giggles.
We go to a restaurant nearby.
Pancho and I order a chicken dish with mole sauce.
Mole is a sauce made from melting chocolate with
more than 10 other ingredients, including chili
peppers and garlic, sesame seeds, and onions.
Everyone drinks a lot of water because the mole
sauce is spicy, but everyone enjoys eating it.

We are in the middle of eating the chicken dish when we hear music playing from outside the restaurant. As the music gets louder, a mariachi comes inside the restaurant. Mariachi is a small band that plays instruments and sings Mexican songs. The mariachi comes to our table and sings a song.
For their last song, they sing the cheerful but sad song, "La Cucaracha."
The tourists must know the song too because they sing along. But do you think the tourists know that "La Cucaracha" means "the cockroach"?
It is a song about the sad reality of poor farmers.

Unfortunately, it is time to go our separate ways.
Pancho gives the tourist boy a piñata as a gift and says,
"Put as much candy as you can inside here."
After saying goodbye, I start feeling sad as I walk away.
I run back and put my hat on the boy's head.
The boy gives me a big smile. I smile back at him.
We wave to each other for a long time.

◇ ◻ **Piñata**

A piñata is a hollow papier-mâché or clay figure that is hung from the ceiling during Mexican children's birthday parties and special occasions. The piñata is filled with candy or toys, and the blindfolded children hit it with a stick until it breaks apart. The children share and enjoy the candy and gifts that fall from the piñata.

When I come home, my grandma asks,
"Juan, did you have fun today?"
"Yes I did, but my heart feels empty."
I tell her everything that happened today without
leaving anything out.
My grandma holds my hands tightly and says,
"Juan, we all have at least one sweet and spicy
memory that we treasure.
These memories are what make our lives wonderful."
Just then, I hear the church bells ringing from
outside the window.
My family holds hands and gives a prayer of thanks.
And like that, my own festival has ended too.

The Story of Mexico as told by Juan

Capital: Mexico City

Language: Spanish

Natural Environment: The country's lands are uneven, with many high plateaus. The capital, Mexico City, is located on those plateaus. People experience a variety of climates because Mexico has mountains, deserts, and tropical rainforests.

In the center of the flag is a drawing of the legend behind how the country was founded.

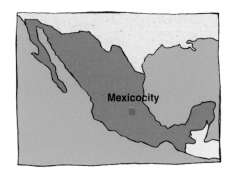

Mexicocity

Where is Mexico located?

Mexico is located in the continent of North America just above Central America.

To the north, it borders the United States; to the south, it borders Guatemala and Belize. To the east, it borders the Gulf of Mexico and, to the west, the Pacific Ocean.

MEXICO

Who lives in Mexico?

The first inhabitants of Mexico were Native Americans. After the Spaniards conquered Mexico, there was a mix of Native American and Spanish people.

Famous Places in Mexico!

In Mexico City, the capital, there is the grand church of Our Lady of Guadalupe, where many people believe the Virgin Mary has shown miracles. One of the main temples of the Aztecs, called Templo Mayor (Spanish for "Great Temple"), is located near the plaza of Zocalo. The Aztecs, well known for their accomplishments and glorious civilization, are the ancestors of the Mexican people.

This is the church of Our Lady of Guadalupe.

Mexico has many ancient ruins. The most famous are the pyramids. Mexico is the country with the most pyramids. Teotihuacan is a global historical site that contains massive pyramids and various temples.

A Mexican person dressed as a skeleton is celebrating "The Day of the Dead" festival.

This is a pyramid in Teotihuacan.

What Festivals are in Mexico?

People in Mexico enjoy having festivals. There is one unique festival called "The Day of the Dead." It is celebrated in early November, and it is the most extravagant festival. People believe that the spirits of their dead family members and friends come to visit them on this day. People dress up in skeleton costumes and prepare food, flowers, and candles to welcome the spirits. The streets are filled with skeleton toys and decorations.

The Story of Mexican Cuisine

A World Heritage Tradition of Mexican Cuisine

On November 16, 2010, UNESCO designated the tradition of Mexican cuisine as a World Heritage. It was the first time that a tradition of cuisine was designated to be worth preserving as a World Heritage by UNESCO. The category includes the way ingredients are gathered, how recipes are passed along, ways in which the food is eaten, and legends behind the food.

People in Mexico believe food is a connection between the land and the heavens. Therefore, eating is a very important ceremony for Mexican people. There are also many legends behind foods. One famous legend says that man was created from corn. Because of the abundance of legends behind Mexican foods and the love Mexican people have for food, it is being preserved and acknowledged as the best traditional cuisine.

The Story of Cacao, the Bitter Tasting Water

Cacao, a key ingredient in making chocolate, is a bean that has been used in beverages and as medicine by Mexican natives. Cacao was valuable enough to be used as money. When the Spaniards first invaded Mexico, they were not interested in the cacao bean after they sampled the cacao sap, saying it produced nothing but bitter tasting water. However, once they began adding sugar to it, they liked the taste and enjoyed drinking it. Although it was first consumed as a beverage, it spread to Europe where it was used to create the chocolate we know today.

The Story of Chili Peppers, Mexico's Spicy Taste

Along with corn, chili pepper is another key ingredient used in Mexican cuisine. Mexican people love chili pepper so much that they sprinkle chili pepper powder on cookies and ice cream and even have beverages that taste of chili pepper. Mexico has a great variety of chili peppers, from ones that numb your mouth to very mild ones.

Habanero

This is the spiciest chili pepper in Mexico. A habanero is not eaten alone; it is used in dishes or to make sauces.

Jalapeno

A jalapeno is not spicy when you first eat it, but it becomes spicy as you keep chewing it. Jalapenos become spicier after they are roasted and dried, and they are found in many Mexican cuisine.

Chili Pepper

Chili peppers are a pepper well known for its spiciness. They come in different sizes and colors, such as red, purple, yellow, green, and black. Sauce made from chili peppers is a famous spicy sauce known worldwide. Chili pepper is ground and mixed with bell peppers, vinegar, and sugar.